Waltham Forest Public Libraries

Please return this item by
the last date stamped.
The loan may be renewed
unless required by
another reader.

2 1 MAR 2008		
	1 4 JUN 2008	- 1 OCT 2010
3 1 JUL 2008		
2 9 AUG 2014	2 6 AUG 2011	
	1 2 SEP 2011	
2 8 NOV 2008	1 7 NOV 2011	
6 MAR 2009	2 4 APR 2012	
1 8 AUG 2009		
	2 8 JUN 2012	
		1 9 NOV 2
2 0 MAR 2010	0 5 APR 2013	
1 9 AUG 2010	3 0 JUL 2013	
	2 2 SEP 2014	

First published in 2006 by
Franklin Watts
338 Euston Road
London
NW1 3BH

Franklin Watts Australia
Hachette Children's Books
Level 17/207 Kent Street
Sydney
NSW 2000

A CIP catalogue record for this book is available
from the British Library.

ISBN (10) 0 7496 6680 3 (hbk)
ISBN (13) 978-0-7496-6680-4 (hbk)
ISBN (10) 0 7496 6693 5 (pbk)
ISBN (13) 978-0-7496-6693-4 (pbk)

Series Editor: Jackie Hamley
Series Advisor: Dr Barrie Wade
Series Designer: Peter Scoulding

Printed in China

To find out more about Malachy Doyle
and his books, please visit:
www.malachydoyle.co.uk

Jack the Giant-Killer

by Malachy Doyle and Graham Philpot

W
FRANKLIN WATTS
LONDON•SYDNEY

Once upon a time in Cornwall, there was a huge and horrible giant.

His name was Cormoran, and he lived up on Saint Michael's Mount.

Every now and again, Cormoran
would come down to the village
and steal the people's cows
and their hogs, their sheep
and their dogs. Soon, they
had hardly any food left.

One of the villagers was
a brave boy called Jack.

"I'm going to sort that giant out!"
said Jack to his friends.

That night, when everyone was sleeping, Jack crept out of the house.

With his spade in one hand
and his horn in the other,
he clambered up the hill.

When Jack got to the giant's lair
he dug a great hole in the ground
at the front of the cave.

Then he covered it with sticks
and straw.

Jack waited by the hole and, as the sun rose, he pulled out his horn and he blew it.

"Who's making all that noise?
I'm trying to sleep!" roared the
giant from inside the cave.

Jack blew his horn again,
even louder.

"If you don't stop now, whoever you are," roared the giant, "I'll come out there and eat you for breakfast!"

But Jack marched right up to the
mouth of the cave, where the
giant was sure to see him,
and blew even louder still.

He bounded to the mouth of the cave and was just about to grab Jack and rip his head off, when ...

"Aaaarrrggghhh!" he yelled,
dropping into the pit.

Before the giant could do a thing
about it, Jack grabbed his spade,
took a mighty swing and whacked
him on the head.

"**Aaarrrggghhh!**" yelled the giant, again. He reached out an arm to grab hold of Jack and pull him into the pit.

But Jack skipped out of the way,
swung his spade and whacked
him once more.

This time he killed the mighty
giant, stone dead. "I've done it!"
cried Jack. "I've saved the village!"

He ran into the giant's
cave, to see what he
could find. There,
gleaming in the corner,
was a treasure chest,
full of gold and silver.

When Jack came back down to the village with the giant's head in one hand and the treasure chest in the other, everyone was amazed.

"Hurrah!" they yelled.

"Hurrah for Jack the Giant-Killer!"
And this was his name, from
that day on.

Hopscotch has been specially designed to fit the requirements of the National Literacy Strategy. It offers real books by top authors and illustrators for children developing their reading skills. There are 37 Hopscotch stories to choose from:

Marvin, the Blue Pig
ISBN 0 7496 4619 5

Plip and Plop
ISBN 0 7496 4620 9

The Queen's Dragon
ISBN 0 7496 4618 7

Flora McQuack
ISBN 0 7496 4621 7

Willie the Whale
ISBN 0 7496 4623 3

Naughty Nancy
ISBN 0 7496 4622 5

Run!
ISBN 0 7496 4705 1

The Playground Snake
ISBN 0 7496 4706 X

"Sausages!"
ISBN 0 7496 4707 8

The Truth about Hansel and Gretel
ISBN 0 7496 4708 6

Pippin's Big Jump
ISBN 0 7496 4710 8

Whose Birthday Is It?
ISBN 0 7496 4709 4

The Princess and the Frog
ISBN 0 7496 5129 6

Flynn Flies High
ISBN 0 7496 5130 X

Clever Cat
ISBN 0 7496 5131 8

Moo!
ISBN 0 7496 5332 9

Izzie's Idea
ISBN 0 7496 5334 5

Roly-poly Rice Ball
ISBN 0 7496 5333 7

I Can't Stand It!
ISBN 0 7496 5765 0

Cockerel's Big Egg
ISBN 0 7496 5767 7

How to Teach a Dragon Manners
ISBN 0 7496 5873 8

The Truth about those Billy Goats
ISBN 0 7496 5766 9

Marlowe's Mum and the Tree House
ISBN 0 7496 5874 6

Bear in Town
ISBN 0 7496 5875 4

The Best Den Ever
ISBN 0 7496 5876 2

ADVENTURE STORIES

Aladdin and the Lamp
ISBN 0 7496 6678 1 *
ISBN 0 7496 6692 7

Blackbeard the Pirate
ISBN 0 7496 6676 5 *
ISBN 0 7496 6690 0

George and the Dragon
ISBN 0 7496 6677 3 *
ISBN 0 7496 6691 9

Jack the Giant-Killer
ISBN 0 7496 6680 3 *
ISBN 0 7496 6693 5

KING ARTHUR STORIES

1. The Sword in the Stone
ISBN 0 7496 6681 1 *
ISBN 0 7496 6694 3

2. Arthur the King
ISBN 0 7496 6683 8 *
ISBN 0 7496 6695 1

3. The Round Table
ISBN 0 7496 6684 6 *
ISBN 0 7496 6697 8

4. Sir Lancelot and the Ice Castle
ISBN 0 7496 6685 4 *
ISBN 0 7496 6698 6

ROBIN HOOD STORIES

Robin and the Knight
ISBN 0 7496 6686 2 *
ISBN 0 7496 6699 4

Robin and the Monk
ISBN 0 7496 6687 0 *
ISBN 0 7496 6700 1

Robin and the Friar
ISBN 0 7496 6688 9 *
ISBN 0 7496 6702 8

Robin and the Silver Arrow
ISBN 0 7496 6689 7 *
ISBN 0 7496 6703 6

* hardback